How Rabbit Lost His Tail

How Chipmunk Got Its Stripes

Why Hummingbirds Drink Nectar

THREE NATIVE AMERICAN POURQUOI TALES

retold by Cynthia Swain
illustrated by Liz Conrad and Jackie Urbanovic

Table of Contents

POURQUOI TALES

What is a pourquoi tale?

A pourquoi tale is a short story that explains why something in the natural world is the way it is. Usually the characters in a pourquoi tale are animals. Sometimes the characters are other objects in nature, such as the sun, the sky, or the sea.

What is the purpose of a pourquoi tale?

Pourquoi tales are explanations of why and how things happen in nature. Pourquoi tales allow us to think about what caused the curious things we see in the world. Pourquoi tales often point out character flaws, or foibles, that people have, such as being boastful, proud, or impatient. In addition, these tales entertain us.

How do you read a pourquoi tale?

When you read a pourquoi tale, pay attention to the title. The title will help you know what question the story answers. Pay attention to the actions of the main characters as well. These actions will cause some type of change in nature. Think about how the events in the tale explain why something is the way it is.

Features of a Pourquoi Tale

The setting is often a key part of the story.

The story is brief. The title is about something in nature.

The main characters are usually animals or objects in nature.

The story presents a problem and a solution that explains why things in nature are a certain way.

The characters' actions cause something to occur, or happen, in nature.

One character has a flaw.

Who invented pourquoi tales?

People have told pourquoi tales for tens of thousands of years. Many ancient cultures, including the Greeks, Chinese, and Egyptians, used these types of stories to explain nature and the universe. Many Native American, African, and Asian storytellers also used these tales to answer questions about the world, such as:

- Why do certain animals look and act the way they do?
- How did Earth, the sun, and the moon come to be?
- Why do the seasons change?

Today, some authors still use this genre to explain events in nature in a fun and imaginative way.

Learn About
NATIVE AMERICAN STORYTELLERS

Background: Prior to 1492, North America was populated exclusively by groups of Native Americans. These first peoples lived closely with nature. Part of their tradition was oral storytelling. Native peoples in North America today still tell their traditional tales explaining the natural world.

"How Rabbit Lost His Tail" was told by the Sioux people. The Sioux homeland covered parts of modern-day Wisconsin, Minnesota, North Dakota, and South Dakota. Sioux women built and owned their family's homes, and cooked and cared for the children. The men were responsible for finding food and defending their families.

"How Chipmunk Got Its Stripes" comes from the Seneca people, who first lived in what is now New York. Long ago, Seneca men hunted, traded, and went to war, while the women farmed and took care of the family and their property.

"Why Hummingbirds Drink Nectar" is a story from the Hitchiti people. The first Hitchiti tribes lived in west Georgia. In the 1700s, the Hitchiti joined other tribes from Georgia and Florida to form the Seminole Nation. The women farmed, cooked, and took care of the children, while the men hunted and went to war to protect their families.

The Seneca people lived in longhouses.

Many Seminole people lived in chickees.

The Sioux people lived in tepees.

Tools Writers Use
Metaphor

A **metaphor** (MEH-tuh-for) compares two things that are alike in one way. Metaphors directly describe something by using the word **is** or **was** rather than **like** or **as**. Writers use metaphors to help readers create pictures in their minds. Notice how the author of these tales uses this type of comparison to describe what something looks, feels, tastes, smells, sounds, or acts like. Authors also use metaphors to show how characters or objects resemble, or represent, something else.

How Rabbit Lost His Tail

R abbit was the most handsome of all the forest animals. He strolled around like a king, with a thick, white robe of fur. Rabbit was not **humble**. He was extremely proud. He knew that his long, bushy tail made everyone jealous.

"Brrr," Deer shivered in the cold. She wished she could have a warm tail. In the winter she would wrap it around herself to keep cozy and warm.

"Whoosh," said Owl. He, too, wanted a long tail like Rabbit. It would help Owl knock out his prey so he could scoop it up easily with his claws. Even Squirrel believed his tail was **puny** compared to Rabbit's big, fluffy, strong tail. "Could I have just one strand of hair from your tail?" Squirrel asked Rabbit. "It is a small thing for you to do. But it would mean the world to me."

"Never could I ever spare a hair! Don't you see? It wouldn't be fair," said Rabbit as he puffed up with pride. He began to sing and dance around. The snow began to fall heavily. It was the coldest winter that anyone could remember.

After hours of showing off his tail, Rabbit grew tired. The snow was a thick, white carpet that now buried his burrow. The stars in the night had hidden from sight. All Rabbit could see ahead of him was a dry branch of tree to rest on. Rabbit quickly fell asleep. He was so **weary** that he slept for days. When he finally opened up his eyes, he saw that the sky was blue and felt that the day was warm.

"Oh, I will find many delicious berries to eat on this bright sunny day," Rabbit said as he stretched his limbs. Now he was wide awake.

But as he stretched, he almost lost his balance. Rabbit looked down and was immediately terrified. The snow had melted away. He was holding on to a branch that might break off any second. Rabbit had to think fast. "Deer, please help me!" shouted Rabbit. "You know how to leap high into the air and never get hurt when you touch the ground. Teach me."

"I cannot," said Deer sadly. "Long ago, we could have been good friends and shared so much. But now it is too late for you to learn."

"Owl, please help me!" moaned Rabbit. "Can't you tell me how you fly wherever you want to go, high or low?"

"I am sorry," said Owl wisely. "Flying is something only birds can do. Still, I could have taught you how to use your tail like a parachute to land softly. But all you wanted to do was show it off."

"Squirrel," pleaded Rabbit, "we are like brothers. We both have wonderful tails and gather food from the forest. Can't you teach me to climb down trees?"

Squirrel smiled sadly and sang his own song to Rabbit. "Never, ever would I dare. Can't you see? It wouldn't be fair."

So, Rabbit had no choice. He closed his eyes and let himself fall to the ground. He was a heavy stone, falling straight down to the ground. As he fell, his tail caught in a branch and was pulled off. That is how Rabbit lost his long tail.

From that day on, all rabbits have had short, little tails. It is a reminder to them to always be **generous** with their friends and not to be selfish or boastful.

Analyze the Characters, Setting, and Plot

- Where did the tale take place? Why is this setting important?
- Who were the characters in the tale?
- What lesson did the main character learn?
- What question does the tale answer?

Analyze the Tools Writers Use: Metaphor

- The author compared the snow to a . . . because . . . (page 7)
- The author compared the falling rabbit to a . . . because . . . (page 9)
- These metaphors use the senses of . . .
- These metaphors create pictures of . . . in my mind.

Focus on Words: Antonyms

The author uses many describing words in this pourquoi tale. Some of the describing words are antonyms, or opposites, such as **warm** and **cold**. Make a chart like the one below. Then reread the tale to find antonyms for the following words.

Page	Word	Antonym	How do you know?
6	humble		
7	puny		
7	weary		
10	generous		

How Chipmunk Got Its Stripes

The morning forest was a feast waiting for Bear's arrival. Today he breakfasted on thousands of ants he found beneath a log. Nearby he saw a tiny chipmunk with a big grin.

"Bear," said Chipmunk. "The ants are scared of you. The bees hide their honey when they hear you roar. Everyone says you are the most powerful creature in the world."

"Yes, I am the biggest and strongest creature around," bragged Bear. "I am the best at everything!"

"Everything?" said Chipmunk with a **chuckle**.

Bear frowned, then roared. "How dare you laugh at me! I am king of the forest!"

The forest fell silent. Everyone was terrified of Bear's bad temper. Everyone but Chipmunk.

"If you are so powerful," said Chipmunk, "then I dare you to stop the sun from shining tomorrow."

"*You* dare *me*?" The ground shook from Bear's laughter. "Of course I can stop the sun."

The challenge was official.

The next morning, it was still dark outside when Bear left his cave and Chipmunk climbed out of his hole. They sat together to see what would happen next.

First, the birds began to sing. Then daylight appeared. Finally, the sun popped up its head and shone brightly.

Chipmunk was a happy little lark. "I won, I won! The sun is more powerful than Bear!"

Bear was not at all happy. In fact, he was **furious**.

He pounced on Chipmunk and pinned him to the ground with his giant paw. "I may not be as powerful as the sun, but I am more powerful than you! You have seen your last sunrise!"

Though Chipmunk was small, he was clever. No one had been able to capture and eat him yet. "Bear, I apologize. Please let me say a final good-bye to the world."

Though Bear was angry, he was not **unreasonable**. He was a fair creature. "Say your good-byes," Bear commanded, "and be quick about it."

"But Bear," Chipmunk gasped. "I need to breathe. Please lift your paw a little."

Bear lifted his paw a tiny bit. It was just enough for Chipmunk to escape.

Chipmunk was no longer trapped. He darted away. Bear lunged, but he could not grab Chipmunk. Bear's sharp claws were just long enough to reach Chipmunk's back, though. *Scratch!*

Chipmunk got away, but not without three long scars on his back. From that day on, all chipmunks have three stripes in their fur to remind them to never, ever make fun of a bear.

Analyze the Characters, Setting, and Plot
- Where did the tale take place? Why is this setting important?
- Who were the characters in the tale?
- What lessons did the characters learn?
- What question does the tale answer?

Analyze the Tools Writers Use: Metaphor
- What did the author say the forest was in the morning? How are these two things alike? (page 12)
- What did the author mean when she compared Chipmunk to a lark? How are these two things alike? (page 13)
- What did the author mean when Bear told Chipmunk "You have seen your last sunrise"? (page 13)
- What mind-pictures did these metaphors create?

Focus on Words: Antonyms
Antonyms are words that have opposite meanings. Antonyms can help you define unfamiliar words. Make a chart like the one below. Then reread the tale to find antonyms for the following words.

Page	Word	Antonym	How do you know?
12	chuckle		
13	furious		
14	unreasonable		

Why Hummingbirds Drink Nectar

Long ago, Heron and Hummingbird used to hunt for fish in the same river. They became friends, but they were very different. One was day and one was night.

Heron was big and slow. His wings were so wide he could fly in the sky forever. Each day, he ate tons of fish.

Hummingbird was tinier than a mouse but she was fast. She could even fly backward as well as forward. But Hummingbird could only eat a few tiny fish a day. She was sure that Heron would eventually swallow up all the fish and leave nothing for her.

So Hummingbird came up with a plan. She would wait for perfect weather and then challenge Heron to a race.

That day finally arrived. The sun was sitting lazily in the sky. The winds were too tired to blow.

"Who is **entitled** to all waters? You or I?" asked Hummingbird.

"The Maker has created Earth for all of us to share," Heron answered. "We do not deserve to rule over any of it."

"You're wrong," Hummingbird huffed. She lifted up her long, pointy beak. "I deserve all the waters because I am the best hunter. I am more clever than a fox and faster than a cheetah. The rivers and lakes should be mine."

Heron laughed at Hummingbird's foolish pride.

Hummingbird grew angry. "I **wager** that I can beat you in a race. Whoever wins will own the waters. Do you accept my challenge?"

Heron did not like to bet, but he sighed and accepted. The two birds agreed that the race would take place over two days.

Hummingbird doesn't want to share and doesn't trust Heron. She is both foolish and proud. The author wants the reader to wonder how Hummingbird's flaws will affect the outcome of the story.

The setting of a pourquoi tale is often important. The author also tells the basic plot, or events of the story. The race gives the characters a reason to interact with each other. We already know that they are opposite types. A contest will make their conflict seem bigger.

The metaphor comparing the flowerbed to a "sea" of daisies is a more colorful way of saying "a lot." It also helps the reader draw a picture in his mind of what is happening and feel like Hummingbird flying around and drinking nectar from flowers.

They would fly over a different forest and river each day. Whoever reached the second riverbank first would win the race and the prize.

Hummingbird **soared** into the sky. Her wings flapped so quickly and hard that a humming sound could be heard throughout the forest. After a while, she could see that she was miles ahead. Unlike Hummingbird, Heron was still on the ground. Then he began to slowly flap his wings, taking his good old time.

Hummingbird grew hungry from all the flapping. She spied a sea of bright yellow daisies below.

She decided to quickly taste the nectar of each flower. The nectar was delicious. It was hours until Hummingbird looked up at the sky. When she did, she saw that Heron was ahead of her.

"Oh no," said Hummingbird. Once again, she flew with all her might until she passed Heron. When night fell, Hummingbird was **exhausted** from flying for so long. She decided to rest.

Heron, however, was well rested. He did not feel at all tired, so he flew steadily, if slowly, through the night.

When Hummingbird awoke, she was hungry again. Now she found a garden of roses. She sipped up all the tasty nectar she could find. She looked into the sky and saw that Heron was nowhere around.

"Heron must have given up," thought Hummingbird. Relaxed and happy that she was about to win, she ate some more nectar. But when Hummingbird finally arrived at the second riverbank, she saw Heron sitting on a tree limb.

Hummingbird was **flabbergasted**. "How did you beat me? I am faster and smarter than you."

Hummingbird's flaws—greed for nectar and overconfidence in her abilities—causes her to lose the race.

The actions of the characters—the outcome of the race—is the reason why hummingbirds today now only drink from flowers instead of eating fish, like herons. This ending, an explanation of something in nature, makes it a pourquoi tale.

Heron was not surprised at all. "Really? Then why didn't you fly all day and night as I did? Why did you spend your time sipping nectar?" Heron inquired.

Hummingbird did not have answers to Heron's questions. She did not know what to say. From that day forward, herons have owned all the rivers and lakes, and hummingbirds have fed only on nectar.

Reread the Pourquoi Tale

Analyze the Characters, Setting, and Plot

- Where did the tale take place? Why is this setting important?
- Who were the characters in the tale?
- What lessons did the characters learn?
- What questions does the tale answer?

Analyze the Tools Writers Use: Metaphor

Find examples of metaphors in the tale when . . .

- the author describes how Heron and Hummingbird are different. (page 16)
- the author describes what the sun is doing and why the winds don't blow. (page 17)
- the author causes you to use your senses and creates a picture in your mind.

Focus on Words: Antonyms

Make a chart like the one below. Then reread the tale to find antonyms for the following words.

Page	Word	Antonym	How do you know?
17	entitled		
17	wager		
18	soared		
18	exhausted		
19	flabbergasted		

How does an author write a

POURQUOI TALE?

Reread "Why Hummingbirds Drink Nectar" and think about what the author did to write this tale. How did she develop the tale? How can you, as a writer, develop your own pourquoi tale?

(1.) Decide on a Question about Nature
Remember, a pourquoi tale answers a question about animals or other parts of nature. In "Why Hummingbirds Drink Nectar," the author wanted to show why herons eat fish and hummingbirds drink nectar.

(2.) Brainstorm Characters
Writers ask these questions:
- Who is my main character?
- What human flaw does my main character have?
- How does my main character show this flaw? What does he or she do, say, or think?
- What other character will be important to my story? How will this character show that he or she does not have the flaw of the main character?

Character	Hummingbird	Heron
Traits	fast; clever; overconfident	kind; slow; steady
Flaw/Asset	feels entitled	wants to share
Examples	says she deserves to rule over the waters	says Earth is for everyone; no one deserves to rule over it

 3. **Brainstorm Setting and Plot**
Writers ask these questions:
- Where does my pourquoi tale take place?
  How will I describe it?
- What is the problem, or situation?
- What events happen?
- How does the tale end?
- Does the tale answer my question about nature?

Setting	a forest
Problem of the Story	Hummingbird is afraid Heron will eat all the fish in the river.
Story Events	1. Hummingbird challenges Heron to a two-day race, saying the winner will own all the waters. 2. Hummingbird flies fast, but she keeps stopping to drink nectar and rest. 3. Heron flies slowly and steadily all day and night.
Solution to the Problem	Heron wins the race, and Hummingbird learns that faster and smarter is not always better. From then on, hummingbirds feed on only nectar instead of fish.

Glossary

chuckle　　　　(CHUH-kul) a quiet laugh (page 12)

entitled　　　　(in-TY-tuld) deserving of ownership (page 17)

exhausted　　　(ig-ZAU-sted) fatigued; very tired (page 18)

flabbergasted　(FLA-ber-gas-ted) very surprised (page 19)

furious　　　　(FYER-ee-us) very mad (page 13)

generous　　　(JEH-nuh-rus) giving; willing to share (page 10)

humble　　　　(HUM-bul) showing respect; not boastful (page 6)

puny　　　　　(PYOO-nee) tiny; very small (page 7)

soared　　　　(SORD) flew (page 18)

unreasonable　(un-REE-zuh-nuh-bul) without clear thought (page 14)

wager　　　　　(WAY-jer) to place a bet (page 17)

weary　　　　　(WEER-ee) exhausted; very tired (page 7)